All About Anime and Manga

Anime and Manga Fandom

Leanne Currie-McGhee

ReferencePoint
Press®

San Diego, CA

© 2022 ReferencePoint Press, Inc.
Printed in the United States

For more information, contact:
ReferencePoint Press, Inc.
PO Box 27779
San Diego, CA 92198
www.ReferencePointPress.com

LIBRARY OF CONGRESS CATALOGING-IN-PUBLICATION DATA

Names: Currie-McGhee, L. K. (Leanne K.), author.
Title: Anime and manga fandom / by Leanne Currie-McGhee.
Description: San Diego, CA : ReferencePoint Press, Inc., 2022. | Series:
  All about anime and manga | Includes bibliographical references and
  index.
Identifiers: LCCN 2021035601 (print) | LCCN 2021035602 (ebook) | ISBN
  9781678202163 (library binding) | ISBN 9781678202170 (ebook)
Subjects: LCSH: Animated films--Japan--Juvenile literature. | Animated
  television programs--Japan--Juvenile literature. | Fantasy comic books,
  strips, etc.--Japan--Juvenile literature. | Fans
  (Persons)--Psychology--Juvenile literature. | Popular culture--Japanese
  influences--Juvenile literature.
Classification: LCC NC1766.J3 C87 2022 (print) | LCC NC1766.J3 (ebook) |
  DDC 791.43/340952--dc23
LC record available at https://lccn.loc.gov/2021035601
LC ebook record available at https://lccn.loc.gov/2021035602

Contents

Connections

Justin Oh, who lives in Singapore, believes that anime not only has provided him entertainment and enjoyment for over a decade but also has helped shape who he is today. Anime is film and video animation that originates in Japan and is defined by vibrant, colorful graphics depicting emotive characters. Anime draws in viewers around the world, of all ages, backgrounds, and personalities, because of the diverse genres and relatable characters. Oh's love of anime began in 2010, when he started watching *Clannad*. He says the anime series about a troubled teen dealing with family issues and struggles helped him deal with his own issues. "There were plenty of characters that I could relate to—introverts, outcasts, people who stayed at home all the time—and scenes that gave me a boost of serotonin and made me feel less alone," Oh explains. "I now had something to look forward to, and I found comfort in the fact that there were real people behind these stories with similar experiences."[1] Anime often lifted Oh's spirits and made him feel less lonely.

Being part of the anime fandom also connected Oh to people with similar views and interests. The many online groups, in-person clubs, and conventions held around the world offered opportunities to share ideas and experiences. "I made like-minded friends in school and through attending conventions like Anime Festival Asia. I felt that I'd finally found a place where I truly belonged, with others who were just as passionate about the same things as me."[2]

Oh's immersion in the world of anime happened fairly quickly. At one point early on he realized that he had watched all 220 episodes of *Naruto* and half of the 500 episodes of *Naruto Shippuden* in just one month. He continues to watch shows, purchase merchandise related to the shows, and attend conventions. Oh's love of anime has even led him to travel to Japan. "As I grew older and finally had the money to spare, I went to Japan for the first time to fully experience the culture first-hand," he writes. "One of the highlights of my trip was visiting the famous staircase where the characters Taki and Mitsuha met in the award-winning anime, *Kimi no Nawa*."[3]

> "I felt that I'd finally found a place where I truly belonged, with others who were just as passionate about the same things as me."[2]
>
> —Justin Oh, anime fan

Connecting Through Experiences

Oh is by no means unique. Like him, many anime fans watch thousands of hours of shows, attend conventions and clubs, and

Devoted fans immerse themselves in the world of anime and manga through cosplay festivals (pictured), clubs, online groups, and conventions. Shared passions often lead to new friends and a sense of belonging.

visit famous anime sites. Most anime fans also share a great love of manga, the graphic novels and comics produced in Japan that are frequently the basis for anime. Around the world, anime and manga fans often become involved in anime- and manga-related activities, both online and in person, to connect with others and build upon their manga and anime interest.

There is no shortage of immersive activities for diehard anime and manga fans. In November 2020, for example, Japan's Kyushu Railway Company began offering rides on a steam train that was designed to resemble the train that plays a central role in the blockbuster anime film *Demon Slayer: Mugen Train*. The film, which opened in October 2020 in Japan and in April 2021 in the United States, is based on a hugely popular manga series by Koyoharu Gotouge. The series features an adolescent boy, Tanjiro Kamado, who fights human-eating demons after most of his family is slaughtered and his younger sister becomes a demon. The anime focuses on Tanjiro's efforts to save passengers riding on the Mugen Train. Devoted *Demon Slayer* fans were able to buy tickets to ride on the Mugen Train replica. While on the train, they could talk to one another, walk around the train, take pictures with staff dressed as characters from the anime, and buy a variety of *Demon Slayer*–themed merchandise. On November 1, 2020, more than seven hundred spectators showed up just to watch the full train make its first trip.

Beyond trains, anime- and manga-themed arcades, stores, cafés, online chat rooms, clubs, museums, and amusement parks are extremely popular among fans. They enjoy all of these venues and activities because of their passion for the characters and stories and the chance to connect with other devoted fans. Anime and manga have been expanding their global reach year by year. Between 2020 and 2021, the market for Japanese manga and anime grew by 20 percent, according to one industry trade group, and that trend is likely to continue. With story lines and characters targeted to people of all ages, genders, and backgrounds, fandom is also on an upward swing as it reaches all corners of the world.

Chapter One

Who Is the Fandom?

On April 15, 2021, people in countries around the world binge-watched hours and hours of anime. This was National Anime Day, established in Japan nearly fifty years ago but now a worldwide celebration of the Japanese art. Streaming services such as Tubi offered several anime shows, past and present, for people to watch for free. In addition to watching, fans shared with others their love of anime on social media with tweets, posts, and videos about their favorite shows and characters. J.P. Cromwell has been an anime fan since kindergarten, has delved into related areas such as *Pokémon* cards, gaming related to anime, and an anime club in high school, and he has continued to watch anime throughout his life. "As an adult, you look back at all this and ask: if you could, would you do this all over again," Cromwell writes. And you know the answer is definitely a yes. . . . It still is fun. And many years from now, you'll still be partaking in this medium. So happy Anime Day."[4]

With COVID-19 still limiting large gatherings in some countries, social media played a large part in celebrating the 2021 National Anime Day. Throughout the day, people posted about their favorite shows, characters, and scenes. In the United Kingdom, Amazon Prime Video, an on-demand streaming service, even gave some fans the chance to have their Twitter profile pictures created in anime style. Amrit Birdi, a London-based artist and award-winning illustrator, transformed the profile pictures for those who were selected. Through all of these posts, passionate fans were able to connect with each other and share their favorites. "It's National Anime Day and I love anime. [It's] brought such great joy to my life," tweeted a fan who goes by the handle Pixel Girl Slays. "Would you add your recommendations on what anime you love and I can add it to my list!"[5] Posts like this occurred worldwide, throughout the day, as the fandom came together to celebrate.

Extensive Fandom

As Japan is the home of anime and manga, it is where fandom originated before extending to the rest of the world. In Japan, the influence of anime and manga can be seen everywhere, including advertisements on trains, shops selling anime- and manga-related merchandise along the streets, people in costumes visiting anime cafés, and billboards lining the highways. Anime and manga are so prevalent in Japan that businesses often include anime or manga icons in their advertising campaigns. "Manga and anime not only often draw inspiration from Japanese daily life, many Japanese organizations also rely on them to communicate or sell," writes Ced Yong, a graphic artist and travel writer from Singapore. "Some cities even use anime to educate, or to honor the achievements of residents, or to promote tourism."[6] As an example, the 2021 Summer Olympics in Tokyo featured several ambassadors from popular manga and anime series. They included Doraemon, a robotic cat from the future, and Astro Boy, the android that gave modern manga its start.

Japan is arguably the center of the anime and manga fandom universe. A 2019 survey conducted by the Nippon Research Center revealed that fully one-third of people living in Japan frequently

read manga or watch anime. But both art forms have expanded their reach far beyond Japan's borders. Globally, anime now accounts for 60 percent of animated television shows, says the Japan External Trade Organization. The popularity of manga and anime is also apparent from how much money these industries generate. In 2019, anime generated approximately $24 billion in revenue, according to the Association of Japanese Animations. This represented a 15 percent increase over the previous year. And in 2020, manga climbed 23 percent above the previous year's sales, resulting in $5.6 billion for the industry. Fans around the world are boosting these industries as manga and anime become significant leisure activities for people.

What Attracts Fans?

One of the reasons why manga and anime attract fans across the world is because their story lines appeal to people of all interests. There are adventure stories, romance, science fiction, drama, and even stories that revolve around cooking, soccer, and skateboarding. Additionally, anime and manga are targeted to people of all ages, genders, and sexualities. *Shonen* is targeted to young men, *shojo* to young women, and *yaqi* and *yuri* to those identifying as LGBTQ, and there are many more stories focused on specific groups of people. As Carlos Ross, an anime and manga reviewer, explains,

> With literally thousands of titles released over the last fifty years, it's like talking about movies or television: there's something for just about everyone. And I think that's what is so appealing about anime and manga: it doesn't seem constrained to use animation to tell a limited set of narratives. It seems like you can find a Japanese comic about anything: a few months ago, I actually tweeted a manga creator who was doing a series on birdwatching![7]

> **"With literally thousands of titles released over the last fifty years, it's like talking about movies or television: there's something for just about everyone."[7]**
>
> —Carlos Ross, anime critic and fan

To meet fan demand, new anime and manga are being created all the time. The Anime News Network notes that it is typical for there to be 30 to 40 new anime releases in Japan every three months. In any given year, it would not be unusual for fans to be able to choose from 150 different anime shows.

Another draw of anime and manga are the well-developed characters in the stories. One of the reasons why the characters are engaging is that they are drawn so their emotions are easily understood. In both manga and anime, the characters' eyes are large and expressive, and their emotions are usually obvious to a reader or viewer. Artists achieve this effect in various ways. Two common techniques used for this purpose are panning, where the camera moves across the scene or character, and zooming, focusing close-up on a character or scene. These techniques help to magnify a character's expressions, actions, and reactions. Because of this focus on character, people find themselves con-

Finding a Respite from the Pandemic

Iréne Schrader, a college student in the Netherlands, grew up with manga and anime—and loved both. But in high school, she turned her focus to academics and her social life, leaving manga aside. Then came college and the COVID-19 pandemic. Schrader's classes went virtual, and she was forced to spend months alone indoors. She turned to her old love, anime, to fill up those hours, to relieve the solitude, and to lessen the stress of the chaos caused by the pandemic. Schrader found that anime helped pass the time in a fun way, while also giving her hope and optimism. "I found solace in watching the continuous selfless bravery that the Survey Corps preserve in *Attack on Titan* to work towards a collective brighter future, Akko's drive in *Little Witch Academia* to achieve her dreams, Gon's undying positive attitude in *Hunter x Hunter*, and the way Izuku focuses on his own growth rather than focus on others' in *My Hero Academia*." Coming back to her childhood passion helped Schrader stay positive during long periods of being on her own.

Iréne Schrader, "Reviving My Love for Anime During a Pandemic," *Sunstroke Magazine*, May 14, 2021. www.sunstrokemagazine.com.

necting with them, which keeps fans involved in the series. "There are many characters that, for one reason or another, grab our hearts to the point where we care about them," writes anime and manga fan Kami Nomi. "Whether it's some goofy, spiky haired kid from *Dragon Ball* with only a pole and a 4 star ball left by his dead grandpa, or a young girl named Sora Naegino with enough passion to fly to the United States from Japan to fulfill her childhood dream, sometimes we get attached to them—and they influence us in ways most mediums can't do."[8]

Many fans have also found parallels with their own lives in the themes explored by anime and manga. For example, in the manga and anime *ReLIFE,* the central character is twenty-seven years old, has been unable to find a job, and wrestles with ways to gain independence from his parents. In the anime *Wonder Egg Priority,* magical wonder eggs make it possible for the characters to help people deal with the dark thoughts that result from being bullied, engaging in self-harm, and other difficulties. Viewers and readers sometimes gain strength or insight into their own lives through these stories. Jenn, a young woman who blogs about anime, is among those who have experienced this effect. Anime, she says, helped her deal with being bisexual and understanding that liking other women was not wrong or bad. "I had a lot of self-loathing because I thought liking girls was ~*evil*~, so seeing anime girls wholesomely crushing on other anime girls made me feel much better,"[9] Jenn writes.

Anime and manga also give people a chance to live out fantasies and escape real life. While watching, they are transported into completely different lives and worlds. "What's the most random story you can think of? There's probably an anime for that. School of compulsive gamblers? Check." writes Peta Hardiman, writer for the Nerd Daily website. "Universe where humans co-exist with any number of mythical creatures? Check. Journeys of a guy who eats a magical fruit and is trying to become the Pirate King? Check. There are no limitations on what worlds or characters exist, it's truly astounding."[10]

"What's the most random story you can think of? There's probably an anime for that."[10]

—Peta Hardiman, a writer for the Nerd Daily website

Who Are the Fans?

Anime and manga attract fans of all ages and from every walk of life. Those who develop a passion for anime and manga often do so during their preteen and teen years. *Sailor Moon*, about a schoolgirl who transforms into a warrior and uses her superpowers to protect Earth from the forces of evil, attracts younger viewers. Young viewers have also been drawn to *Pokémon,* which revolves around a boy who trains fictional creatures called Pokémon, as he journeys to become a Pokémon master.

Older teens are drawn to stories that feature characters of similar age who are in situations like themselves, such as dealing

with school, but with added fantasies like supernatural powers. *Naruto, My Hero Academia,* and *Fruits Basket* are just some of the many anime and manga series that appeal to older teens. "I like action/in-your-face and sports anime because the characters are funny. My favorite anime is *My Hero Academia*. It's about kids with superpowers battling villains. It's in your face and funny."[11] explains Zoe Clevenger, a teen anime fan.

Manga and anime do not necessarily lose their appeal once teenagers become adults. Many manga and anime series explore themes that appeal to adult sensibilities. "I am a huge anime fan and I started watching anime when I was like 19 years old, basically as a teenager, I am 26 now and still a regular viewer and I am not planning to stop watching them," explains fan Vikram Chandhary. He writes,

So, what makes adults watch Japanese animation? There are far more reasons than I elaborate here. Anime shows are not just for entertainment, they are entertaining, but they mostly convey much deeper meaning and life lessons. First of all, anime has a bucket full of genres like—action, adventure, fantasy, comedy, magic, Drama, slice of life, supernatural, horror, mystery, psychological, romance, sci-fi and many other subgenres. What I am trying to tell here is that the possibilities are unlimited.[12]

In addition to all ages, anime and manga draw fans from all races and ethnicities. Since the 1960s, when anime was first introduced in the United States, Black Americans have been drawn to the increasingly popular genre. "I went to a predominately Black school for nearly four years, and if you didn't watch *Naruto* on Saturday evenings prior to school on Monday, you would ultimately

Inspiration for Professional Athletes

Larry Ogunjobi, a defensive tackle for the Cincinnati Bengals, grew up with anime. He felt that many of the characters helped him on his journey to becoming a professional athlete. Ogunjobi was overweight as a kid, but he dreamed of one day playing football. Ogunjobi believed in himself and knew that hard work would pay off because he saw this occur with his favorite characters, such as Naruto. "You have a character and things don't go their way . . . do they quit or do they push through it?" explains Ogunjubi. "I always took those kinds of life lessons and nuggets that anime [shows] have in them, and my appreciation just grew and grew into a real love for anime." Eventually he received five college scholarship offers.

Over the years, Ogunjobi has encountered other professional athletes who found inspiration in their favorite anime characters. "Overall, I'm slowly starting to see more people, more pro athletes show their fandom. We're able to put ourselves in the same shoes as some of these characters. There have been times in a game where I have put myself in the mindset of a main character from one of my favorite anime," Ogunjobi explains.

Quoted in Crunchyroll, "Crunchyroll All-Stars: Larry Ogunjobi on Going to Conventions from Anime Expo to Japan," May 5, 2021. www.crunchyroll.com.

be left out of lunchroom conversation for the first half of the week," recalls Channler Twyman, a writer and anime fan. As he explains,

> If you go to conventions like MomoCon in major urban cities like Atlanta, Black people are there in abundance! Now, stars like Michael B. Jordan are voicing their love for the medium, YouTubers such as AfroSenju and RDC World1 have amassed huge subscriber counts for their anime-related content, and a multitude of Black influencers tweet gifs and constantly make references towards their favorite shows.[13]

When asked what attracts them to *Naruto*, many Black American fans cite the fact that the popular anime features characters who overcome adversity. These characters resonate with these fans because they too have experienced and overcome obstacles in their lives.

All of these different types of people make up the fandom, and they come together to celebrate anime and manga in different ways. What they share is a love of the characters, stories, and settings of anime and manga. They are united in this passion and connect because of it.

Chapter Two

Connecting with Others

Fans of anime and manga often develop a close connection to those who share their interests. As a result, these fans will strike up friendships and meet up virtually and in person to bond over their collective interests. These connections are evident in the many anime and manga clubs, conventions, and social media groups throughout the world.

Student Clubs

Student clubs are a popular way to connect with peers who share common interests. This holds true for fans of anime and manga all the way up through college. At these clubs, fans gather to watch anime and to discuss anime and manga. They also develop friendships, which can become long-term relationships. Lauren Orsini, a web developer and anime blogger, met many like-minded friends and her future husband through her college anime club. In 2018, she posted on Twitter, "9 years ago I asked the anime club prez on a date and 5 years ago today I married him."[14]

Some school clubs go further than discussion groups. At Mc-Donough 35 Senior High School in New Orleans, Louisiana, the anime club encourages a high level of student participation and creativity. They have done this through cosplay, which involves creating and dressing up in costumes of favorite manga and anime characters. "We have a good mix of kids that are involved from all levels," says Donald Hess, the African American studies and journalism teacher who started the club. "The students were able to design their own cosplay costumes and attend Wizard World Comic Con. They took hundreds of pictures because everyone loved their costumes so much. They had a blast just being able to be in that environment." Strong student interest has made it possible to expand the club's offerings. Hess explains, "Now, we're even opening up a comic book lounge in the library with hundreds of comic books for kids to read during lunch to hang out and just decompress."[15]

Clubs also offer a way for college-age fans to connect and share their appreciation for anime and manga and to learn more about Japanese culture. The Brooklyn College Anime Manga Club has been active for years. Before the pandemic, members gathered twice a week to watch anime, read manga, exchange opinions about whatever they were viewing and reading, and just generally enjoy each other's company. Members also typically shared a Japanese meal and held discussions about different aspects of Japanese culture. During the pandemic, they continued to gather—but, like most everyone else, they switched to online platforms. Members say the club helped them explore their passion for anime and manga and helped them enjoy their college years. "I wanted to find a place on campus that I felt comfortable in," club president Wayne McIntosh says. "I was a brand new student, so I didn't know anyone, and I liked the atmosphere of [the club]."[16]

Conventions

Another way to meet fellow fans is through anime and manga conventions that take place every year in countries around the world.

They attract thousands of passionate fans by offering discussion panels, screenings, artist appearances and signings, merchandise, cosplay, and more. One of the biggest conventions, Comiket (or Comic Market), takes place in Japan. It attracted more than 700,000 fans in 2019. Other popular conventions include Anime Expo in Los Angeles; 350,000 people attended that convention in 2019. Manga Barcelona, in Spain, also draws big crowds; it attracted more than 150,000 fans in 2018. Many smaller cities and towns host their own conventions, allowing fans to connect with each other and keep up with the latest developments in anime and manga. Although most conventions were halted in 2020 and 2021 because of the pandemic, planning for future conventions has begun in some countries.

In 2019, Anime Expo was a four-day celebration of all things anime. Thousands of fans waited in long, winding lines just to get in. Once inside, they encountered rows of elaborate exhibits previewing upcoming releases and showcasing anime merchandise, people wearing bright, elaborate cosplay costumes, and interactive anime sets where fans could take pictures of themselves. Exploring further led fans to Artist Alley, an entire section of the convention where colorful anime art by independent artists was on display. Fans also visited the entertainment hall, which included cosplay competitions, gaming, and local music. Crowds packed in to see exclusive screenings of premieres, including *Pokémon: Mewtwo Strikes Back—Evolution* and season four of *My Hero Academia.* At night, there were packed concerts, including a performance by renowned Japanese musician and composer Yoshihiro Ike. Joined by fifty musicians, Ike performed his well-known musical masterpieces from numerous anime and game soundtracks. Even with days to attend, fans were never at a loss to see something new, with over four hundred exhibits, five hundred artists, and nineteen premieres from which to choose.

Throughout the world, there are many other, smaller conventions where fans can engage in similar activities. They attend panels where writers, artists, actors, and others discuss how the shows are created. They participate in costume contests, listen to live music performances, and take photos with professional cosplayers. Best of all, fans engage with people who share their enthusiasm for anime and manga. "Anime convention is [a] beautiful thing. I think that you should attend, if you like anime in general or have been an adamant anime supporter, it is [an] amazing thing to find like-minded people enjoying the same attributes,"[17] explains Zak Osman, an anime fan from England.

Some even develop long-term relationships with people they meet at conventions. This is what happened to Claire Zito. Zito's passion for manga and anime began in the fourth grade, and today, in her twenties, anime and manga are still a part of her life. This includes attending conventions; early on, she learned that conventions are a great way to meet people who share her passion for anime. "I have attended them since I was 11 years old," Zito explains. "I participated in a

> "Anime convention is [a] beautiful thing. I think that you should attend, if you like anime in general or have been an adamant anime supporter, it is [an] amazing thing to find like-minded people enjoying the same attributes."[17]
>
> —Zak Osman, anime fan

Virtual Viewing

For many anime fans, much of the fun is watching it with other fans and commenting while they watch. During the COVID-19 pandemic, getting together to do so was more difficult; as a result, fans discovered virtual viewing. For example, Netflix has a Chrome browser extension that one can download called Netflix Party, which allows friends to watch shows simultaneously, on their own devices, and chat at the same time. Another browser extension is Metastream, which allows friends to video stream from sites such as YouTube, Hulu, Crunchyroll, and Twitch, and everyone can watch together while chatting. Some fans even made their own apps to watch together because they missed the interaction. "My friends and I missed the feeling of watching anime together during quarantine, so we made . . . a website to allow us to watch videos together as if we were viewing the same screen," wrote a user on MyAnimeList. "Not only did these sites allow people to connect during the pandemic, but virtual viewing also makes it possible for anime friends who do not live near each other to watch together."

Actinrocket, "I Made a Website to Watch Anime with Friends!," MyAnimeList, May 23, 2020. https://my animelist.net.

lot of social media groups related to anime and its fandoms. . . . Instagram and Twitter have huge followings for all things Japanese pop culture. I was hooked as soon as I discovered people just like me went to these conventions. I met my best friend at one in 2016, and it turned out we lived in the same neighborhood!"[18]

Character Cafés

Fans in Japan can also meet and interact at character cafés. These cafés are specifically themed with characters from anime and manga, serve drinks and food tied to the themes, are decorated in theme, and add other specific touches that relate to the manga or anime. Whereas some character cafés have permanent locations, others pop up for limited periods of time. In some instances, their appearances are tied to new releases of anime or manga. In April 2021, for instance, the Detective Conan Cafe opened for several months in seven locations in four Japanese cities. The café openings coincided with the release of *Detective Conan: The Scarlet Bullet*. This is the twenty-fourth movie of the Case Closed series, which features a high school detective who, after being transformed into a child, tries to solve the mystery of the kidnappings of top executives who have a developed a super-conducting train. The cafés, which resembled the 1950s American diner theme of the series, offered Detective Conan–themed food and drink, original merchandise, and special gifts for visitors.

More permanent character cafés can be found in Osaka and Kyoto, but Tokyo—Japan's capital city of nearly 14 million people—is the character café capital of the world. Pokémon Café, which opened in 2018, is one Tokyo's character cafés. It features Pokémon-themed food, such as buns and cakes made to look like the series' characters. For instance, the café features Jigglypuff-shaped cheesecake. Food is served on plates shaped like the character Pikachu.

Character cafés provide a fanciful venue for manga and anime fans to commune with their favorite characters and sometimes even feel like they are part of the action. When a new season of the anime series *Cardcopter Sakura: Clear Card* began in 2018, a pop-up

Pokémon Café in Tokyo attracts customers with fake food displays (pictured) that reflect some of the real menu items. The menu features Jigglypuff-shaped cheesecake and Pikachu curry, among other items.

Matchmaking Through Anime

Anime is such a passion for some people that they only want to date and marry other anime fans. For this reason, there are matchmaking apps and websites available for anime fans to find a like-minded love interest. The anime dating website MaiOtaku, which started in 2009 and is used worldwide, is one such site. Members, who pay to join, are asked to list their favorite anime in the personal information questionnaires. Through the use of filters and other advanced search features, users can connect with people who share enthusiasm for anime in general or even for specific genres or stories. One user, Megan, says this site allowed her to meet someone she is now dating. "I [have been an] anime lover since always and I want to share this interest with people like me," Megan writes. "I have a few like-minded friends but maiotaku.com allowed me to meet a potential partner who is also [an] anime fan."

Quoted in Perfect.is, "MaiOtaku.com Review 2021," 2021. https://perfect.is/dating/en/www.maiotaku.com.

character café surfaced in Tokyo. It reflected the popular anime in which a middle school student named Sakura finds magical powers after freeing a set of magical cards. One of the featured items on the menu was Sakura's bento box. Bento boxes are essentially Japanese-style lunch boxes that contain a meal for one, with separate compartments for each item in the box. Those items can be simple or elaborate. In *Clear Card*, Sakura's bento boxes sometimes included rice balls, an omelette, and strawberries. These and other items featured in her lunches were included in the café's bento box.

Social Media Interaction

Finally, like people everywhere, anime and manga fans are connecting with each other on social media. TikTok, for instance, is a favorite for those who want to offer video commentary on episodes, make video montages of favorite scenes, share cosplay of themselves, and more. Subscribers can comment on these videos and engage with each other.

At times, fans even create and promote social media trends. This happened with the manga and anime series *JoJo's Bizarre Adventure*. In this series, characters often strike dramatic poses. Fans started doing the same and then posting videos of themselves in these poses, accompanied by the song "JoJo Pose" by Apollo Fresh. By February 2020, videos featuring the song on TikTok exceeded 1.5 billion views.

Social media is also used to share artwork and music related to anime and manga. Many fans use Instagram to share photos of merchandise, artwork, or cosplay with other fans, who then can comment on the posts. On Spotify, where one can select music to listen to and make playlists, people can share their playlists privately with friends or publicly with anyone on the platform. Anime and manga fans use Spotify to develop playlists of music associated with their favorite shows, series, or characters. "One of my favorite pastimes is to make a playlist on Spotify of songs I think the anime characters would listen to. I know it sounds lame, but it's fun!"[19] explains teen Zoe Clevenger, a fan of anime such as *My Hero Academia* and *The Promised Neverland*.

To engage in real-time conversations with multiple people online, fans can meet up in chat rooms or on message boards on various sites. For example, Crunchyroll, a website completely dedicated to anime and manga, features groups specific to shows or manga that people can join and then chat with one another. Several other anime and manga websites provide similar options.

Whether in person or online, fans of anime and manga have several methods to engage with other fans, and many do so. This adds to their enjoyment of the shows and stories, turning their interest into a social activity. Anime and manga creators know this and find more ways for them to connect, ultimately leading to more viewership and readers.

> "One of my favorite pastimes is to make a playlist on Spotify of songs I think the anime characters would listen to."[19]
>
> —Zoe Clevenger, anime fan

Chapter Three

The Rise of Cosplay

From the moment you walk in the door of any anime or manga convention, you are likely to see a Monkey D. Luffy or two, a few Tanjiro Kamados, a couple of Satoru Gojos, some Madokas, and several Urarakas. These are all characters in well-known and popular manga and anime. Some of the costumes have a minimalist feel; a fan might wear a character's familiar hat or sword or carry a notebook, for instance. Other costumes mimic the character down to the smallest details. Many of the costumed fans dress as their favorite characters because it is fun—and because everyone around them also thinks it is fun to see and be seen. Some are in it for the competition; they put their artistry up against the work of others to see which costumes boast the most impressive fit and details. Some take part in cosplay masquerades, where participants parade across a stage and sometimes even present prize-winning skits. Others pose for keepsake photographs in settings that reflect scenes from their favorite manga or anime.

Whether or not fans dress up, cosplay is a major part of anime and manga fandom. Besides conventions, cosplayers can be found at in-person meetups and on social media. Cosplay allows fans to become a part of their favorite shows and stories and to interpret and personalize the characters for themselves. "Cosplay is not just about picking a costume and dressing up," writes Victoria Karambu, a blogger who contributes to the website Comic Book Resource. "It is more about understanding the character and giving life to the costume. It is also about being drawn into a magical world where fans can become their favorite character."[20]

> "Cosplay is not just about picking a costume and dressing up. It is more about understanding the character and giving life to the costume."[20]
>
> —Victoria Karambu, blogger

Why Do People Love Cosplay?

Cosplay is one of the most popular ways to express enthusiasm for anime and manga. It can be done by anyone, and the cosplayer's age does not matter. What matters is using imagination and creativity to develop a costume that represents your own take on a character. "Cosplay isn't always about looking EXACTLY like the character you're cosplaying, but rather how you portray them on yourself specifically! It's always lovely to see people's positive reactions to how you look in a certain cosplay,"[21] says one cosplayer.

Many cosplayers specifically incorporate their own physical features or other characteristics into their cosplay characters. Terry Hall is male, African American, an adult—and a huge anime fan who also enjoys cosplay. No matter which character he portrays, his race, age, and other physical features become part of his cosplaying. "When I look at characters in anime, I more so think of them as to how they relate to me, not really about their race. That is part of why I cosplay anyone no matter what,"[22] says Hall. He has appeared as Himiko Toga, a female character from *My Hero Academia,* and Yuno Gasai, the female protagonist from the manga *Future Diary*.

Although Hall cosplays for fun, he also does it for money. He is a professional cosplayer, meaning people hire him to appear in costume at events such as anime conventions. Mariah Mallad is also a professional cosplayer. She cosplays Rin, a petite character from the anime *Daughters of Mnemosyne*. Mallad notes that she does not have Rin's petite frame, but she likes to cosplay as her because of the character's strength and power. Looking exactly like the character is not the point of cosplaying, says Mallad. The goal for many cosplayers is to interpret the character in their own way. Thus, the costume will usually have some of the most recognizable elements of the character's outfit, accessories, makeup, and hairstyle, but many cosplayers also add other elements that fit their interpretation of that character.

Another reason people love to cosplay is the positive attention they get from other anime and manga fans. When cosplaying, particularly at a convention, people often come and talk to the

Like cosplayers everywhere, these Dragon Ball *cosplayers get to experience being part of their favorite stories and interpret and personalize the characters for themselves.*

Comfortable Cosplaying

Although the look of cosplay attire is important, many who cosplay offer this advice: make sure the costume is comfortable. Whether a professional cosplayer or just wearing it for fun at a convention, a costume that is uncomfortable will make for a miserable time. Rachael Lefler cosplays and writes a blog that covers a range of information, including comic books, science fiction, and cosplay tips. She is extremely detailed with her clothing, makeup, hair, and props when in cosplay, but she always recommends that people consider comfort when they create their attire. "Choose comfort over exactly matching the anime," Lefler recommends. "Your character wears 9-inch stilettos because it is a fantasy world where that does not cause agonizing foot pain. You're not in that world, unfortunately. You can get flats or shorter heels in the same color, still look like the character, and your feet will thank you. The same goes for impossibly big wigs or improbable dresses and weapons."

Rachael Lefler, "Help! 10 Tips for Scared and Confused New Cosplayers," HobbyLark, November 2, 2019. https://hobbylark.com.

cosplayer about their costume and typically compliment them on it. These interactions often lead to discussions about the character and the manga or anime series. The cosplay helps the person attract people who are interested in the same genres and shows as they are.

Cosplay has also helped people through difficult times, giving them something positive to focus on. Chris Minney's love of anime and cosplay helped him recover from a period in his life that involved drugs, alcohol, and poor health. Dressing as his favorite characters, who were strong in spirit, inspired him to become fit and healthy. His dedication to cosplay has garnered him invitations to appear at events and conventions around the world. In addition to these appearances, he will cosplay specifically to cheer or help another person who is experiencing difficulties. "A few months back I was told about a kid who had lost a family member. His favorite character was Goku [from the anime *Dragon Ball*] so I was asked to record a message for him to help bring a bit of light to his situation," writes Minney. "I got into my Goku cosplay and gave him the words I wished I had when I experienced my first loss (and from the hero I most admired)."[23]

Professional Cosplayers

For some, the love of anime and manga cosplay can lead to a career of dressing up. Many cosplay professionals either have a background in graphic arts or design, or they have developed these skills over years of assembling costumes, applying make-up, and creating accessories. These professionals make their living dressing as anime and manga characters and appearing at conventions, special events, and parties.

Stella Chuu began to cosplay while in high school and became more serious with it after she graduated from college in New York. While growing up, Chuu loved watching anime such as *Dragon Ball Z* and *Shadow Skill;* in college, she became the president of the anime club. "I decided to dive super deep into cosplay, because it just looked so cool when I went to conventions with my anime club," Chuu explains. "And I just thought if I learn how to make my own costumes maybe something cool can come from this; maybe I could travel more, maybe I can meet cool people."[24]

Chuu not only traveled and met people, but she also became so successful as a cosplayer that she makes more than $100,000 a year dressing up. Chuu owns over two hundred costumes that she uses for various conventions. Examples of these costumes include Battle Angel Alita, a warrior who wears black leather from

"I just thought if I learn how to make my own costumes maybe something cool can come from this; maybe I could travel more, maybe I can meet cool people."[24]

—Stella Chuu, professional cosplayer

Cosplayers who earn a living by attending conventions spend endless hours developing and perfecting their costumes. One such cosplayer has created more than two hundred costumes, including one for *Battle Angel Alita* (pictured).

a manga comics series of the same name, and Valus, a warrior from the video game *Shadow of the Colossus*. Although she is doing what she loves, Chuu emphasizes that it takes a lot of marketing and effort to achieve this level of success. Before attending an event, she will spend hours on her hair, makeup, and costume and will then post pictures to her more than three hundred thousand Instagram followers. Even though Chuu is not sure how long she will continue this as a full-time career, it has provided her a lot of fun and adventure.

Cosplay to Power

Most cosplay takes place online or at live social events, but a few devoted cosplayers have mixed their hobby with their professional lives. In the spring of 2021, Lai Pin-Yu won election to Taiwan's legislature. At twenty-nine years old, she became the legislature's youngest member. During the election campaign, she spoke out about issues such as traffic, noise pollution, and gender equality. She also brought her love of anime into the campaign—and then into office. At one campaign event, she walked on stage in a red bodysuit and bright orange pigtails—looking like Asuka Langley Soryu from the manga *Neon Genesis Evangelion*. When she won the election, she posted a photo of herself dressed up as Sailor Mars, a ruler of Mars from the manga *Sailor Mars*. Pin-Yu feels that the younger generation is looking for legislators who are relatable and represent their interests. This is why she felt comfortable bringing her cosplay and anime hobby into her political life.

Social Media

To gain a following, Chuu often posts her cosplay on social media. Many other cosplayers, professional and amateur, also share their attire on social media. Social media allows anime and manga cosplayers to display their characters, show off their specific takes on these characters, and engage in conversations with others about their cosplay. Among the most popular forums to display and discuss cosplay are TikTok, Instagram, and Facebook.

For some, sharing their cosplay online not only leads to new interactions with other fans but also to new confidence in their artistic abilities. Ana Nguyen (who uses the pronouns they/them/theirs)—a theater, film, and television student at the University of California, Los Angeles—found that cosplay on TikTok helped to build confidence in their artistry, especially during the pandemic, when interaction with other people was so limited. Nguyen, who often cosplays male characters from *My Hero Academia*, gained more than five hundred thousand followers during this time. The characters Nguyen likes to cosplay the most are Shota Aizawa, a high school teacher, and Keigo Takami, a superhero. Nguyen tried new areas of interest with their cosplay, including comedy, and the positive reception led to different ways of expressing their creativity. Nguyen often develops skits to satirize the characters. "I get comments all the time and they're like 'Wait, you're really funny,'" Nguyen says. "I was like 'Wow, nobody's ever validated my ideas before. I didn't know that I had anything to offer to the world.'"[25]

Like Nguyen, other imaginative cosplayers have attracted large followings on social media. Eleanor Barnes's innovative take on cosplay has resulted in more than 1.1 million followers on Instagram. Her interest in anime began with *Pokémon* when she was ten years old. Her enthusiasm for anime and manga grew as she watched the anime series *Ouran High School Host Club* and read the manga *Death Note*. While still in school, she often dressed up as her favorite characters. For instance, she put her hair in pigtails like Sailor Moon or wore knee socks like Misa Amane from *Death Note*. By 2014 she was using her Instagram account to post photos of herself in different looks, including those inspired by anime, with detailed lighting, clothes, and makeup. This eventually led to her own makeup Instagram account, where she used only makeup and wigs to create head shots of anime, manga, and Disney characters. "I took that inspiration [of dressing up in character] to the next level, posting editorial beauty renditions of well-known anime characters and toying with the idea of full cosplay. Nowadays, I tend to post content that lands somewhere in the middle," explains Barnes. "99 percent of my photos are self-shot headshots rather than full body pictures, which allows me to make sure that the wigs and makeup and what little of the outfit you can see in the final digital image are either super true to canon or a fresh twist on an animated character."[26]

In preparation for a convention, cosplayers in Hong Kong work on their costumes, hair, makeup, accessories, and props. Many cosplayers do their own sewing or find needed items in thrift stores.

Cosplay Meetups

Sharing cosplay in person is also an option for many anime cosplayers. Aside from conventions, where cosplay is prevalent, there are cosplay meetups hosted across the world. People can find these on social media and websites, including Meetup and Facebook. At these meetups, people wear anime and manga cosplay, and they share ideas about how to create costumes, where to shop, and even how to build accessories. For example, in 2018 the Seattle Makers, a group that hosts a place and tools for creating and building, hosted a cosplay meetup for people to learn how to build a Live Action Role Play (LARP) sword, a padded mock weapon used for pretend combat with sound effects.

In Louisiana, there are cosplay meetups as well as an organization that brings cosplayers together. Louisiana Cosplayers is open to all cosplayers, including those whose focus is anime and manga. Through this organization, cosplayers connect online and in person to discuss progress with individual development of costumes, help with designing a concept, construct costumes, and share the best places to buy cosplay accessories. Its Facebook group has more than two thousand members, many of whom met for regular and holiday gatherings (in costume, of course)—except during the COVID-19 pandemic, when in-person activities were suspended.

How to Cosplay

For many, part of the enjoyment of cosplay is researching and preparing the attire. To begin, a person who wants to cosplay needs to determine what character they want to portray. Most choose characters that they admire or identify with on some level. Next, they should carefully research the character's physical appearance, attire, and personality. All of these, plus the cosplayer's own personal take on the character, will help them develop an idea for the costume.

Seasoned cosplayers suggest planning out the costume and determining what clothing, accessories, makeup, wigs, and other props are needed. Whereas some sew or build props on their own, others buy premade clothes and accessories. Longtime cosplayer Mia Moore sometimes makes her own costumes, but when she decided to dress up as Taiga Aisaka from the manga and anime *Tora Dora*, she bought most of the items she needed. When she buys instead of makes her costume and accessories, she often finds some of what she needs at thrift shops. For this costume, Moore purchased penny loafers and a sword on eBay, a white shirt from the Goodwill thrift store, and the skirt and jacket from another secondhand store. She bought the wig, which was cut and styled, at full price. Pulling all of these elements together let her achieve the look she desired for Taiga Aisaka.

Many cosplayers find they acquire new skills through the process of creating their costumes. As Claire Zito became more involved in developing her costumes, she discovered new abilities. "It is incredibly diverse and creative," Zito says. "It inspired me and countless others to learn to draw, sew, style wigs, and create their own stories."[27]

Wearing costumes that they have designed and created from scratch or pieced together from store-bought elements can be very satisfying. This is one of the reasons why so many people engage in cosplay. The other reason is the camaraderie that develops among cosplayers. Cosplay is a way for many anime and manga fans to celebrate, in a creative way, their favorite stories and characters with others who share their passion.

Chapter Four

What Is an Otaku?

People who spend a lot of time reading manga and watching anime, decorating their rooms with anime- or manga-themed items, meeting up with others to watch anime, squirreling away all sorts of details about different manga and anime series, and posting comments online about story arcs and characters would, by many accounts, be considered *otaku*. Otaku are people who are, more or less, obsessed with anime and manga. They have incorporated these arts into most every facet of their lives.

The word *otaku* did not originally refer specifically to those who live and breathe anime and manga. It was initially used to describe anyone with an obsession—from video games to celebrities to food. Around the 1970s, as interest in anime and manga blossomed in Japan, an increasing number of fans started attending conventions, often in costume. Fascination with all things anime and manga grew. But not everyone was enthralled by this make-believe world or the attention it was being given by members of the Japanese public. In a 1983 article, the Japanese writer Nakamori Akio described these superfans as otaku. He did not mean it to be a compliment. He viewed them as obsessive and antisocial. The negative connotation of otaku continued in Japan over the next decade. In 1989, it was even used to describe a serial killer named Tsutomu Miyazaki. He became known as "the Otaku Murderer" after it was revealed that he had a large collection of anime and horror videos.

Despite the negativity initially associated with the word, the anime and manga otaku subculture in Japan grew. Increasing numbers of Japanese fans of anime and manga gathered at conventions, in clubs, and in other social situations to celebrate these arts. The many public events and social gatherings slowly changed attitudes about the otaku, who gradually came to be seen in a more positive light. Over time the term lost most of its disparaging meaning and instead became better known as a description of people with an intense passion for anime and manga. In a 2018 survey of Japanese women ages fifteen to twenty-four by Shibuya109 lab, a Japanese market research company, 28 percent of respondents who were heavily into anime and manga described themselves as otaku. As the term lost its negative connotation, more people in Japan became comfortable being associated with otaku culture.

Otaku Meccas

The otaku subculture grew so much that certain areas of Tokyo became known as "otaku meccas." These areas buzz with anime- and manga-themed shops, restaurants, and events and have become a magnet for costumed fans as well as sightseers. Although Japanese otaku were the first to frequent the otaku meccas, fans from other countries started to seek them out as the popularity of anime and manga spread worldwide.

One of the most famous of the Tokyo otaku meccas is Akihabara. Once known for its electronics shops and appliance stores, Akihabara, located in the Chiyoda district of eastern Tokyo, is made

Akihabara (pictured) is one of the most famous of the Tokyo otaku meccas. The brightly lit streets are lined with video game arcades, billboard advertisements, manga cafés, and stores selling all sorts of manga and anime merchandise.

up of several streets that boast business after business devoted to all things manga and anime. When exiting the train station at Akihabara, the first thing travelers are likely to see is a nine-story-tall red-and-yellow building filled with anime-related shops. Beyond that are brightly lit, crowded streets lined with retro video game arcades, colorful billboard advertisements, manga cafés, and stores with manga and anime figurines, dolls, posters, CDs, toys, and nearly every other piece of manga and anime merchandise available. Sightseers will also find maid cafés, where staff wear the maid outfits that are seen in anime series such as *Blend S, Black Butler,* and *Kaichou wa Maid-sama*. On any given day, costumed people walk the streets, meet up with other fans in the cafés, and play anime-related video games at the arcades.

Another hot spot for otaku gatherings is Otome Road in Ikebukuro, a commercial district in northwestern Tokyo. Like Akihabara, although smaller as it is just one street, it has anime-related shops and cafés, with otaku gathering to visit these spots.

Celebrating Fictional Birthdays

Sana, a Japanese fan of Rengoku (also known as the Flame or Fire Hashira character in *Demon Slayer*), is a super otaku. Her enthusiasm goes way beyond conventions and cosplay: she celebrates the birthdays of her favorite characters. And she does this by covering every surface of her room—floors, walls, and ceiling—with images of Rengoku and all sorts of Rengoku-related merchandise. "It's not until you zoom in that you can start to differentiate the individual elements that are covering the walls, floor, and even the ceiling of the room: a massive amassment of acrylic standees, plushies, pins, and cards all in the image of Sana's beloved Fire Hashira," writes Casey Baseel, who lives in Tokyo and writes for Sora News. How Sana will celebrate Rengoku's birthday in 2022 is anyone's guess.

Quoted in Casey Baseel, "Brain-Breaking Photos from a Super Otaku's Birthday Shrine to Her Favorite Anime Character," Sora News, May 14, 2021. https://soranews24.com.

This area is more tailored to female manga and anime fans, featuring shops with manga romance stories, female costumes, related merchandise, and butler cafés, which are similar to maid cafés but have male butlers instead of female maids. "Since it's a girls' paradise, you can see many girls doing cosplay more publicly than in Akihabara. Also, people can go shopping for girls' goods and activities such as buying Yaoi (Boys Love) manga, costumes, or dropping by the butler café," says a writer for the tourism website Fun! Japan. "However, guys can also visit there to learn about otaku culture, enjoy the atmosphere, and see rare cosplays, too!"[28] As with Akihabara, over the past few decades the area has also grown in popularity with anime and manga fans from outside of Japan.

Embracing the Fashion and Merchandise

At these otaku meccas, one can see that part of being an otaku in Japan includes embracing anime and manga culture through fashion and accessories. Character-themed T-shirts, jackets, sweatshirts, phone cases, and backpacks are among the biggest sellers.

Taylor Hall is a self-proclaimed otaku in the United States who proudly shows off her anime and manga hobby. Hall grew up watching *Pokémon*, *Sailor Moon*, and *Naruto*. By the time she reached high school, her passion for anime was all-encompassing. "By my senior year of high school, I have completely embraced being an otaku," explains Hall. "I had anime all over my notebooks for school, I made friends with people who fully accepted me being an otaku and were even fellow otakus as well. When I went out with friends or out in public, I had clothes on about anime. I started collecting anime plushies, keychains, backpacks, etc."[29] In college, she continued to watch anime every day, read manga daily, and wear anime-themed clothes. She even decorated her room with anime posters and plushies.

Some otaku do not stop there; some decorate their entire house with anime and manga paraphernalia. Agnes Diego and Joey Binsinger live in Japan; their apartment is decorated with all sorts of anime- and manga-themed items. Both are well-known on YouTube—Diego, who has nearly 3 million subscribers, is "Akidearest," and Binsinger is "The Anime Man." Both Diego and Binsinger frequently post videos related to anime and manga fandom and appear as invited speakers at conventions. The two have filled their apartment with anime- and manga-themed merchandise. Anime figurines, stuffed animals, posters, manga artwork, and even an anime jigsaw puzzle decorate the apartment. Their shelves are filled with manga comics and anime DVDs. "And here is my doujin

> "I had anime all over my notebooks for school, I made friends with people who fully accepted me being an otaku and were even fellow otakus as well."[29]
>
> —Taylor Hall, an otaku in the United States

[self-published manga] corner, where I tore out a lot of doujins just for some wallpaper,"[30] Diego says as she gives a tour on YouTube. Diego surrounds herself with anime- and manga-related items so that her house reflects her personality.

Creating as an Otaku

Being otaku is not just about spending money on clothing, posters, and backpacks. Some otaku mine their creative streak by crafting figurines, designing clothing, painting, and even by cooking foods that celebrate their favorite characters and stories. Rich Duffy started ed designing and making anime-themed clothes even before he had heard the term *otaku*. "I made orange Dragon Ball shirts with fabric paint long before they appeared in stores," he says.

Duffy, who moved to Japan to be a teacher and has lived there for years, has immersed himself in anime culture and considers himself to be otaku. He noticed that as Japanese otaku become immersed in their anime and manga, they become inspired to create. "Cosplay, fan fiction, fan games, music, doujinshi [self-published

Some otaku mine their creative streak by crafting figurines, designing clothing, painting, drawing, and even by cooking foods that celebrate their favorite characters and stories. Some of these even turn into money-making ventures.

Otaku Watching Shows about Otaku?

Otaku subculture is so entrenched in Japan that some artists have created anime that focus on the lives of otaku or feature otaku as characters. Among these are *Lucky Star,* an anime that features a girl who experiences problems at school because of her passion for anime and video games. Another example is *Genshiken*, which focuses on members of an otaku club. Additionally, in *Outbreak Company*, the main character is a young otaku who gets a job as a general manager of an entertainment company because of his vast knowledge of anime and manga, but he is then kidnapped and awakens in a fantasy world.

manga], and other creative activities empower otaku," writes Duffy. "They foster participation and ownership of the beloved series. Japan's plethora of hobby specific magazines cover plastic model kits, illustration, customized game systems, and cosplay."[31]

Otaku find a variety of ways to express their creativity and enthusiasm for anime and manga. Zoria Petkoska's medium is food. While at university in Japan, she began cooking anime-themed foods—that is, foods that are featured in various anime or manga. Initially, she focused on typical Japanese foods eaten by on-screen characters. This includes ramen, which is a Japanese noodle soup, and melon pan, which is a Japanese pastry covered in a thin layer of crisp cookie crust. After a while, she decided she wanted more of a challenge. Petkoska decided to take part in a cooking challenge organized by the Tokyo Survival Channel, an online travel website that she writes articles for while living in Japan. Every month, the channel issues challenges to its writers to help them explore Japan and its culture. "Eating like an anime character is a

"Cosplay, fan fiction, fan games, music, doujinshi, and other creative activities empower otaku."[31]

—Rich Duffy, a teacher in Japan

A latte offers a canvas for anime art. Some otaku foodies specialize in making foods that look like anime or manga characters while others focus on items that characters eat or drink in the stories.

great way to drag fantasy out of the screen and into your daily life. Yes, I can always munch on melon pan or pocky, or stuff my face with ramen, but Tokyo Survival Challenge has something trickier in mind," writes Petkoska. "They challenged me to cook 5 anime foods from anime about cooking, in less than a week, recreating the recipes and the look of the dish."[32]

The challenge included recipes specifically made by characters in anime and manga that revolve around food and cooking. Among the foods Petkoska attempted were Japanese curry and naan from *Shirokuma Café,* a manga that features a café run by a polar bear, and *yakisoba* bread from *Yakitate!! Japan*, a manga about a boy's quest to make a national bread for Japan. After this, Petkoska felt compelled to try more and moved on to cocktails. Specifically, she began to mix cocktails made in *The Bartender*, an anime about a bartender who is a master at making drinks. Petkoska shared pictures and descriptions of her works on her blog, for other otaku, or anyone interested in Japanese culture, to enjoy.

Becoming a Weeb

For those living outside of Japan, being an otaku can lead them one step further to becoming a "weeb," also known as a "weea-bo." A weeb is someone who becomes intensely immersed not just in manga and anime but also in Japanese culture as a whole. This includes the Japanese pop music known as J-pop, Japanese food, Japanese fashion, and even learning the language.

Justin Oh, who lives in Korea, started out as an anime fan, beginning with *Clannad*, an anime about a teenage boy dealing with family issues. Over the next decade, Oh watched thousands of hours of anime, including *Clannad: After Story*, *Koe no Katachi*, and *Violet Evergarden*. A self-professed otaku, he attended conventions and made trips to Tokyo to see anime and manga sights. His interest in manga and anime then evolved into a thirst to learn more about Japanese culture. It began with J-pop. "On top of that, I became more immersed in Japanese culture as a whole. My interests soon went beyond just J-pop and anime—from trying my hand at making Japanese food . . . to learning the language."[33]

Whether an otaku in Japan or a weeb in Korea or the United States, these subcultures are attracting more people, and today many are proud to be a part of them. To Oh, who was teased about his love of anime as a kid, this is a good sign. He is glad to see greater acceptance of anime and manga otaku and weebs; he hopes that other otaku, like himself, are able to embrace who they are. "Most importantly from my journey with anime thus far," Oh explains, "I've learned that we should never discriminate against others based on their passions—even if it's something 'weird' or 'crazy.' One should not be ashamed of their hobbies, and while it does take time, accepting yourself for who you are is the most important step into adulthood."[34]

> "I've learned that we should never discriminate against others based on their passions—even if it's something 'weird' or 'crazy.' One should not be ashamed of their hobbies."[34]
>
> —Justin Oh, anime fan

Chapter Five

Artistic Expression

Watching anime and reading manga have led many in the fandom to their own artistic pursuits. Of these, some fans create for fun and to share with the community, but for others, they find their artistic pursuits lead them to a career. In both cases, anime and manga are what inspired them and led them to find their own talents.

Creative Explorations

For those who love to write, there is fan fiction. Fan fiction is fiction inspired by a series, character, or show. Writers develop their own stories that revolve around those shows or characters. Often fans are inspired to share these stories and do so through websites such as Wattpad, Archive of Your Own, and various message boards. "I love writing about my favorite characters and my favorite worlds and even after the series or characters are gone from the big screen, or when the game or book is over, the characters and the worlds still hold a special place in my heart," writes Chloe Gilholy, who writes anime fan fiction, with *Pokémon* being one of her favorite inspirations. "Through writing fanfiction, they become my friends as we explore different territories."[35]

Others in the fandom express their takes on anime and manga through drawings, paintings, and graphic arts software. Some draw or paint the characters in their own style, adding or altering features as they see fit. Others draw the characters as shown in the series but place them in different situations or settings with new story lines. Fan art gives people a chance to try their hands at developing something new, but with a base to start with as they draw, paint, or use a medium of their choice. "Sometimes it's the idea of taking those series out of their usual zones and doing different takes on them. . . . I learn something new with every piece I do," explains Carilus, an anime fan and creator of fan art. "I make it a point to learn a new method or technique with every piece or improve on elements I think can be improved on instead of just churning them out. Fanart just gives me a vehicle with ready-made characters upon which I can practice my techniques of composition and skill."[36]

"Fanart just gives me a vehicle with ready-made characters upon which I can practice my techniques of composition and skill."[36]

—Carilus, creator of fan art

Using Technology

Other artistic endeavors inspired by manga and anime include the development of projects using the latest technology. Many fans develop short videos using either clips and scenes from shows or original skits based on these shows; they then post these on YouTube, TikTok, and other sites. Common among these videos are ones where creative fans splice together various clips from a favorite show or shows and add music in the background. This type of video is known as an anime music video (AMV). Fans who do this learn to use video editing software, such as CapCuts and

Video Star, to develop the videos as they edit anime and music available online.

Jay Naling, who is known as "Koopiskeva" on YouTube, is a well-known AMV creator, with over eight thousand subscribers. He has been making AMVs for over a decade based on the shows that most interest him. One of those shows is *Neon Genesis Evangelion*, an anime story that revolves around an in-

Some devoted fans create their own anime music videos, post them on social media, and develop a following. One well-known creator has made videos about characters from Neon Genesis Evangelion *(pictured),* among other anime shows.

troverted teenage boy who helps save Earth from destruction by bonding with a giant humanoid robot of near-godlike power. Koopiskeva created an AMV about one of the show's characters, Rei Ayanami, an introverted young woman who is the pilot of a giant *mecha*, or humanoid robot, named Evangelion Unit 00. Shawn, a writer, blogger, and fan of anime and manga, describes Koopiskeva's AMV about Rei Ayanami as "possibly the most perfect encapsulation of the haunting existence Rei has. In four minutes, you essentially get an insight into the character, thanks solely to clever editing and a perfect song choice."[37] Longtime creators like Koopiskeva have honed their craft so their videos look professional and can often be mistaken for original anime. Whether a longtime creator like Koopiskeva or a person just starting out in video editing, technology-loving anime and manga fans often find satisfaction in the challenges of making AMVs.

Podcasts provide another forum for creative expression. Anime and manga fans are sharing their thoughts about the latest stories and characters in various podcasts. Among the most popular are *Project: M.A.N.G.A.* and *Anime Out of Context*. *Project: M.A.N.G.A* is hosted by four manga fans; its focus is manga geared toward male teens. Each week the hosts discuss, review, and analyze the latest manga titles and other related topics. The *Anime Out of Context* podcast takes a different approach. It features an anime fan named Shaun Rollins who introduces new shows to Remington Chase, an anime neophyte. The podcast features Shaun and Remington watching the shows and then discussing their reactions. This allows listeners to hear different perspectives on the latest creations. These podcasts allow fans of manga and anime a new way to express their own thoughts and ideas while sharing them with others.

Hip-Hop Inspiration

Although many anime and manga fans express themselves through their artistic endeavors as amateurs, some professional artists have incorporated, or even based their works on, anime and manga. In particular, several hip-hop musicians have been inspired by anime and manga and have developed songs and videos that show these influences.

Rapper, songwriter, and producer Kanye West is a longtime fan of anime and has discussed how it has influenced different aspects of his work. For example, his video for the song "Stronger" (from the album *Graduation*) is inspired by the 1988 anime film *Akira*. Set in a dystopian Tokyo, Akira revolves around a motorcycle gang of thrill-seeking teens who accidentally stumble upon a secret government-run project dealing with telekinetic powers in children. West declared *Akira* to be "the greatest animation achievement in history."[38] The music video includes bright reds and oranges and futuristic, dystopian images and scenes reflected by the anime. West has tweeted and talked about how *Akira* has been his biggest creative inspiration.

The influence of anime can be seen in the work of other rappers too. Wu-Tang Clan, an early hip-hop group, released raps that included references to *Dragon Ball Z*. More recent artists, including XXXTentacion, FulMetalParka$, and Ski Mask the Slump God have done the same. *Dragon Ball Z* is one of Ski Mask the Slump God's favorite anime. In his 2018 song "Lost Souls," he includes a reference to the Destructo Disc, a razor-sharp disc used by Krillin, a talented and powerful martial artist in *Dragon Ball Z.*

Playing for Anime

Professional musicians also can be directly involved with anime by developing, producing, and performing music for the shows. These musicians often grew up as anime fans and use their musical talents and love of anime to help bring the shows to life. Whether instrumental or vocal, the music adds to the style of the anime.

The Japanese singer LiSA made her major debut in 2010 when she sang songs for the anime television series *Angel Beats!* On the show, she was the voice of one of the singers in the fictional band Girls Dead Monster. Her songs have also been included as the theme music for the anime shows *Fate/Zero*, *Sword Art On-*

From Fan to Head of an Anime Studio

Arthell Isom, a Black American, discovered a love of anime as a child and was particularly inspired by *Ghost in the Shell*, an anime film based on a manga about a cyborg public-security agent who is hunting a hacker. Isom knew, as a child, he was meant to create anime. To achieve this goal, he attended San Francisco's Academy of Art University and graduated in 2005. However, his dream was to create anime in Japan, and he knew he had to get there. Isom moved to Japan and eventually was accepted at the Yoyogi Animation School, one of Japan's largest and oldest anime and design schools. Graduating from Yoyogi put him on the path to becoming the art director and chief executive officer of Japan's first Black-owned anime studio. Isom cofounded D'ART Shtajio with his twin brother, Darnell, and animator Henry Thurlow in 2016. The name *Shtajio* combines the Japanese phrase *shtaji ga daiji*, which means "the foundation is important," and *sutajio*, which means "studio." His goal was to create a studio that uses both Eastern and Western ideas and themes in their animation. Some of the anime the studio worked on are *Overlord*, *Tokyo Ghoul:re*, and *JoJo's Bizarre Adventure: Golden Wind*. For Isom and his brother, following their path to Japan resulted in the fulfillment of their childhood dreams.

line, and *Demon Slayer: Kimetsu no Yaiba*. When singing, LiSA tries to connect with the characters she represents to express them through song. Her song "Dawn," released in 2021 as the opening theme song for the anime series *Back Arrow*, rose to number eleven on the Japan Top 100.

The series revolves around a young man who has lost all of his memories and mysteriously appears in Lingalind, a continent that is surrounded by a wall that the inhabitants consider to be a god. The only thing the young man (who calls himself Back Arrow) knows is that he has come from outside the wall. The show follows his quest to restore his memories and discover who he is while dealing with the warring nations inside Lingalind. The song's beat and lyrics add to the feeling of anticipation and uncertainty as the story progresses.

Fashion Expression

Although many anime and manga fans have turned to art, writing, music, and videos to express their visions, others have found creativity in fashion. Rather than dressing as a character, as cosplayers do, these individuals put together inventive outfits with anime and manga roots. Anime characters often wear bright colors and have vibrant features, so the fashion may include brightly colored hair, bold makeup, and clothing ranging from schoolgirl uniforms to robes, depending on the genre of anime. Lizzie Bee, a manga fan, finds she expresses herself best wearing *gyaru*-styled fashion. *Gyaru* is typically characterized by bleached or dyed hair, tanned skin, colorfully painted nails, and bold makeup—which together resemble the characters Yuzu, the protagonist of *Citrus*, and Anaru of *Anohana: The Flower We Saw That Day*. Over the years, Bee has developed her own unique look based on anime fashion and *gyaru* style. "My Gyaru journey has been long but I'm so comfortable in my skin now and feel like I have finally discovered my own Gyaru style," writes Bee. "I wear the clothes that make me happy and there's nothing more important than that."

Lizzie Bee, "My Gyaru Style; The Beginning, Middle and Now," Hello Lizzie Bee, September 22, 2019. www.hellolizziebee.com.

Composers have also been drawn to anime. Hiroyuki Sawano is well-known in Japan as a composer of musical scores for anime. He watched many series while growing up and realized early on that he wanted to be a composer. In his work as a composer, he has made music for many anime series, including *Attack on Titan,* which is about a civilization where the last humans live, and *Kingdom,* which is a fictional account of early China. In all of his works, Sawano's goal is to develop music that evokes emotions that draw audiences into the scenes.

On Display

Professional artists have also found success in developing art with distinct links to manga and anime. These artists, many of whom are based in Japan, develop art based on popular culture and mass media. They are generally known as pop artists.

Takashi Murakami is among the most famous anime-influenced pop artists. His pieces have sold for millions of dollars. Growing up in Japan, he was a huge fan of anime and manga. He even intended to become an animator, but he eventually majored in Nihonga, a style of Japanese painting. Murakami, who calls himself an otaku, ties many of his creations to anime and manga. One of his anime-inspired pieces consists of 9-foot-tall (2.7 m) figures crafted out of fiberglass and synthetic resin. The figures resemble anime characters with their large eyes and elongated limbs. In several of his works, Murakami features a character he has named "Mr. DOB." This character takes inspiration from the video game *Sonic the Hedgehog*, the manga series *Doraemon*, and the *yokai*, which are strange creatures from Japanese folklore. Murakami's otaku-influenced art has been showcased around the world.

Another famous Japanese pop artist whose work has been influenced by anime is Hiroshi Mori. His work combines elements of various artistic styles, including those found in anime, video games, the work of American artist Andy Warhol, and even portraits by European Renaissance artists such as Leonardo da Vinci. Mori likes to combine different styles of art in one piece, such as Renaissance portraits with anime characters. In 2018, Mori discussed some current pieces in his exhibition: "My experience in Japanese culture helps me to integrate gaming, comics and anime with iconic pop art from the West. Another combination that's interesting to me is the integration of Japanese anime characters with masterpieces from famous painters such as Claude Monet which are being shown in the current exhibition in Hong Kong."[39] Mori's mash up of styles, both in influences and medium, have led to a devoted global following.

"My experience in Japanese culture helps me to integrate gaming, comics and anime with iconic pop art from the West."[39]

—Hiroshi Mori, artist

Professional Comic Creator

Some devoted fans even develop careers as creators of original manga and anime, transforming their talent and drive into works others will love. Hiro Mashima became addicted to all types of manga as a youth in Japan, and he knew he wanted to be a manga artist, or *mangaka*, when he grew up. Among his greatest influences were the art of Toriyama Akira, the creator of *Dragon Ball* and *Dragon Ball Z*, and Yoshinori Nakai and Takashi Shimada, also known as Yudetamago, the creators of *Ultimate Muscle*. What drew Mashima to these series were their fierce battle scenes and their victorious protagonists. Like many artistic fans, Mashima's creativity initially was expressed in his amateur works, but then he used these to build a career. "I created a 60-page original work that I took into editors to review," Mashima explains. "Then I won an amateur manga artists' competition. After a year, I made my official debut in 1999."[40] From that point on, he became well-known for his manga series. Mashima's *Rave Master,* which focuses on a teen who is working to save the world, ran for thirty-five volumes. *Fairy Tale*, another of his works, focuses on a guild of wizards who are fighting against evil guilds. Mashima's childhood love has stayed with him, and it is why he is passionate about his career.

Like Mashima, Emmy-nominated Rebecca Sugar turned her childhood passion into a career that she loves. As a kid, Sugar watched lots of cartoons and anime. One of the anime shows she liked most was *One Piece*, a series about the adventures of Monkey D. Luffy, a teen whose body becomes like rubber after he accidentally eats a Gum Gum Devil Fruit. Wearing his trademark straw hat, Luffy and his pirate crew sail all over the world in search of the priceless treasure called "One Piece." Sugar eventually created *Steven Universe*, an animated show that ran on Cartoon Network from 2013 through 2019. It melded her love of superheroes and anime with magic and LGBTQ themes and characters. "I love making animation for kids," she says. "I think they're such a great audience. Their imaginations are so huge. It's difficult to imagine giving up an audience that's so open, and so

Rebecca Sugar turned her childhood passion for anime into a career. Melding her love of superheroes and anime with magic and LGBTQ themes and characters, she created Steven Universe, which ran on Cartoon Network from 2013 to 2019.

STEVEN UNIVERSE
CREATED BY REBECCA SUGAR

imaginative that you can throw wild concepts in, and wild visuals in, and have your audience be really immersed. I just really love doing this work."[41]

Anime and manga have inspired creativity in countless others as well. Whether or not they pursued this creativity professionally, their love of anime and manga inspired them to discover and advance their artistic skills and imagination.

Source Notes

Introduction: Connections

1. Justin Oh, "My Parents Thought Loving Anime Was a Phase but I'm Still a 'Weeb' 10 Years Later," TheSmart Local, April 17, 2021. https://thesmartlocal.com.

2. Oh, "My Parents Thought Loving Anime Was a Phase but I'm Still a 'Weeb' 10 Years Later."

3. Oh, "My Parents Thought Loving Anime Was a Phase but I'm Still a 'Weeb' 10 Years Later."

Chapter One: Who Is the Fandom?

4. J.P. Cromwell, "An Ode to Anime: Happy National Anime Day," Artes Collective, April 15, 2021. https://artes collective.com.

5. Pixel Girl Slays, Twitter, April 15, 2021. https://twitter.com/PixelGirlSlays/status/1250847969097678848.

6. Ced Yong, "Manga and Anime Culture in Japan: It's Everywhere!" Wander Wisdom, January 8, 2021. https://wanderwisdom.com.

7. Carlos Ross, email interview with the author, April 26, 2021.

8. Kami Nomi, "5 Reasons People Love Anime," MyAnimeList, February 14, 2016. https://myanimelist.net.

9. Jenn, "Anime Escapism, or Why My Depressed Ass Watched So Many Japanese Cartoons," Welcome to Hell Zone!, October 21, 2019. https://jennshellzone.com.

10. Peta Hardiman, "10 Reasons You Should Be Watching Anime (If You Aren't Already)," Nerd Daily, August 8, 2018. https://thenerddaily.com.

11. Zoe Clevenger, email interview with the author, May 1, 2021.

12. Vikram Chandhary, comment on "Why Do Some Adults Also Like to Watch Anime?," Quora, 2019. www.quora.com.
13. Channler Twyman, "The Invisible Underdogs: The Relationship Between Black Folks and Anime," Anime Feminist, February 8, 2018. www.animefeminist.com.

Chapter Two: Connecting with Others
14. Laruen Orsini, Twitter, June 2, 2018. https://twitter.com/laureninspace/status/1003052910832504832?lang=e.
15. Quoted in InspireNOLA Charter Schools, "The Inspired: The Soul of InspireNOLA," January 20, 2020. https://inspirenola.exposure.co.
16. Quoted in Mary Zakharova, "BC'S Anime and Manga Club Stay Connected in Virtual World," *Brooklyn College Vanguard* (blog), April 14, 2021. https://vanguard.blog.brooklyn.edu.
17. Zak Osman, comment on "Should I Go to an Anime Convention," Quora, 2017. www.quora.com.
18. Claire Zito, email interview with the author, April 28, 2021.
19. Clevenger, interview.

Chapter Three: The Rise of Cosplay
20. Victoria Karambu, "The Ten Most Popular Female Anime Character Cosplays Last Year," July 12, 2020. www.cbr.com.
21. Quoted in Kami Nomi, "How to Cosplay: Great Advice from 12 Cosplayers," MyAnimeList, March 23, 2016. https://myanimelist.net.
22. Quoted in Kendra Beltran, "Black Anime Cosplayers Discuss Representation in Anime," Cosplay Central, February 17, 2021. www.cosplaycentral.com.
23. Chris Minney, "Cosplay Motivation: Making People Happy," *Be More Shonen* (blog), 2019. https://bemoreshonen.com.
24. Quoted in Tom Huddleston Jr., "This 29-Year-Old Makes Six Figures a Year as a Professional Cosplayer," CNBC, October 8, 2018. www.cnbc.com.
25. Quoted in Kari Lau, "Theatre Students Use TikTok as Outlet for Expression of Creativity," *Daily Bruin*, April 28, 2021. https://dailybruin.com.
26. Quoted in Janae Price, "Meet the Black Anime Cosplayers Blowing Up on Instagram," *Vice*, May 2, 2019. www.vice.com.
27. Zito, interview.

Chapter Four: What Is an Otaku?

28. Mon, "Ikebukuro Otome Road: A Wonderful Holy Land for Otaku Girls," Fun! Japan, July 27, 2020. www.fun-japan.jp.
29. Taylor Hall, "I Am a Girl, I Love Anime, and I Am Not Ashamed of It," Odyssey, www.theodysseyonline.com.
30. Akidearest, "Tour of My Otaku Room in a Japanese Apartment," YouTube, February 16, 2019. www.youtube.com/watch?v=ZUcLKX5dcM4.
31. Rich Duffy, "How I Learned to Stop Worrying and Love Being Otaku," Tofugu, June 6, 2016. www.tofugu.com.
32. Zoria Petkoska, "Making Anime Food in Real Life: 5 Dishes, 1 Week, 1 Obsessed Otaku!," Tokyo Survival Channel, August 10, 2020. www.kunugi-inc.com.
33. Oh, "My Parents Thought Loving Anime Was a Phase but I'm Still a 'Weeb' 10 Years Later."
34. Oh, "My Parents Thought Loving Anime Was a Phase but I'm Still a 'Weeb' 10 Years Later."

Chapter Five: Artistic Expression

35. Chloe Gilholy, "Why I Love Writing Fanfiction," Geeks, 2017. https://vocal.media/geeks.
36. Carilus, comment on "Why Do You Draw Fan Art?," Reddit, 2017. www.reddit.com.
37. Shawn, "A Quick Guide to Anime Music Videos," Anime Whiz, August 14, 2020. https://animewhiz.com.
38. Quoted in Amid Amidi, "Kanye West Proclaims 'Akira' as the 'Greatest Animation Achievement in History," Cartoon Brew, September 1, 2018. www.cartoonbrew.com.
39. Quoted in Isabel Wong, "Japanese Artist Hiroshi Mori Turns Fine Art Masterpieces into Anime," Tatler, May 17, 2018. https://hk.asiatatler.com.
40. Quoted in Deb Aoki, "Hiro Mashima," Live About, February 11, 2019. www.liveabout.com.
41. Quoted in Daniel Holloway, "'Steven Universe' Creator Looks Back on Her Groundbreaking Series as It Comes to a Close," Variety, March 18, 2020. https://variety.com.

For Further Research

Books

Matt Alt, *Pure Invention: How Japanese Culture Conquered the World*. New York: Crown Illustrated Vision, 2020.

David Watts Barton, *Japan from Anime to Zen: Quick Takes on Culture, Art, History, Food . . . and More.* Berkeley, CA: Stone Bridge, 2021.

Hector Garcia, *A Geek in Japan: Discovering the Land of Manga, Anime, Zen, and the Tea Ceremony.* North Clarendon, VT: Tuttle, 2019.

Robert M. Henderson, *Quick Guide to Anime and Manga*. San Diego: ReferencePoint, 2022.

Evangeline Neo, *A Manga Lover's Tokyo Travel Guide: My Favorite Things to See and Do in Japan.* North Clarendon, VT: Tuttle, 2019.

Internet Sources

Theo J. Ellis, "If You Want to Know Why People Like Anime So Much, Here's the Answer!," Anime Motivation, 2021. https://animemotivation.com.

Gita Jackson, "Anime Conventions Changed Culture Forever. COVID Could End Them," *Motherboard* (blog), Vice, February 3, 2021. www.vice.com.

Akira Kyles, "'I Kind of Find Myself Through Cosplay': Fayetteville's Cosplay Culture Embrace Expression," *Fayetteville (NC) Observer*, June 22, 2021. www.fayobserver.com.

Rachael Lefler, "How to Be an Otaku: Your Guide to the Subculture," ReelRundown, June 5, 2019. https://reelrundown.com.

Rachel Moulden, "Sharean Morishita: Manga & WebComics Creator Interview," Fandom Spotlite, July 15, 2021. https://fandomspotlite.com.

Luke Plunkett, "Early Anime Fans Were Tough Pioneers," Kotaku, November 22, 2016. https://kotaku.com.

Thomas Wick, "Anime's Growth in America Encourages Diverse Viewpoints," *Pitt News* (Univ. of Pittsburgh), April 12, 2018. https://pittnews .com.

Websites

AnimeCons.com

https://animecons.com

AnimeCons.com provides a worldwide listing of anime conventions. It provides links to register for the conventions as well as information on the times, locations, and guests.

Anime News Network

www.animenewsnetwork.com

This website provides news about anime, manga, and video games. The site also includes reviews of anime and manga and press and convention information.

Crunchyroll

www.crunchyroll.com

With over 3 million subscribers, Crunchyroll provides anime and manga to view on its website. Additionally, the website provides the latest news regarding manga and anime and forums to discuss the art forms.

MyAnimeList

https://myanimelist.net

MyAnimeList is the largest online database and community for anime and manga. Users can create lists of anime and manga from the database. This website provides the latest anime- and manga-related news. Additionally, there are groups and clubs on the website where fans can connect.

Index

Picture Credits

About the Author

Leanne Currie-McGhee has written educational books for nearly two decades. She lives in Norfolk, Virginia, with her husband, Keith; children, Grace and Sol; and dog, Delilah.